ME

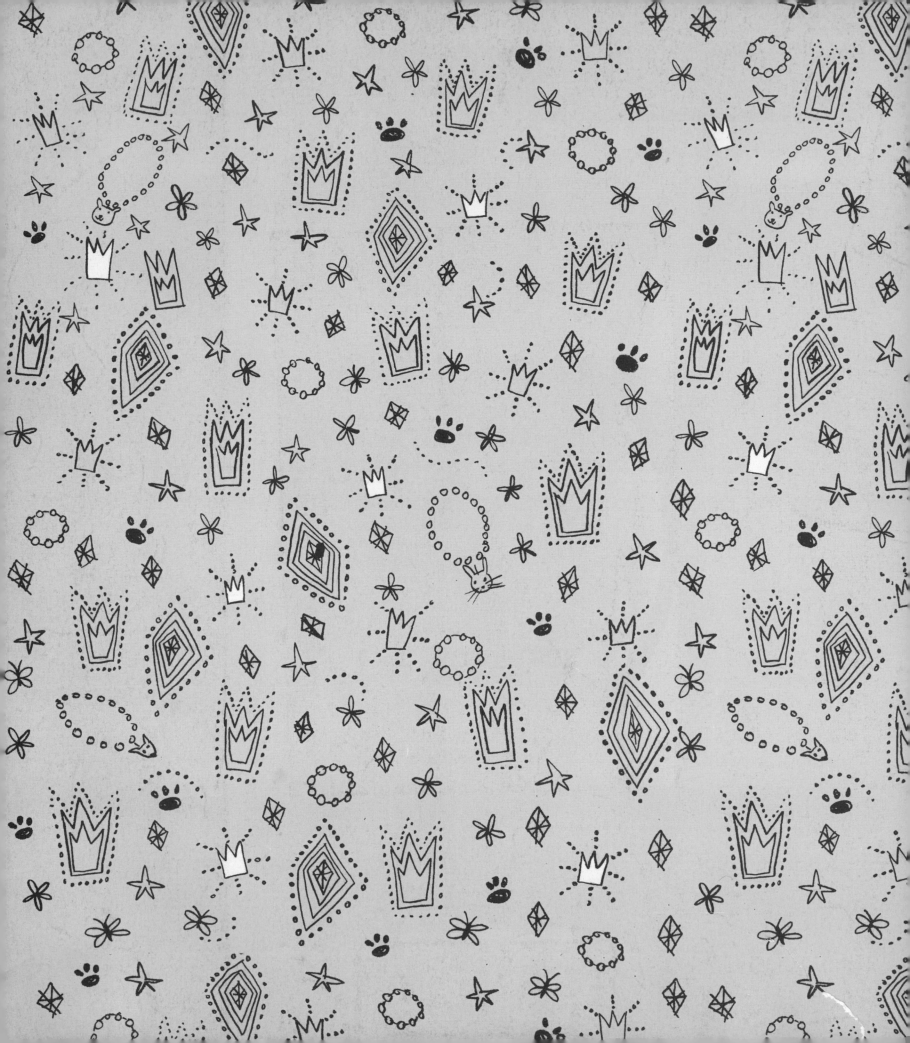

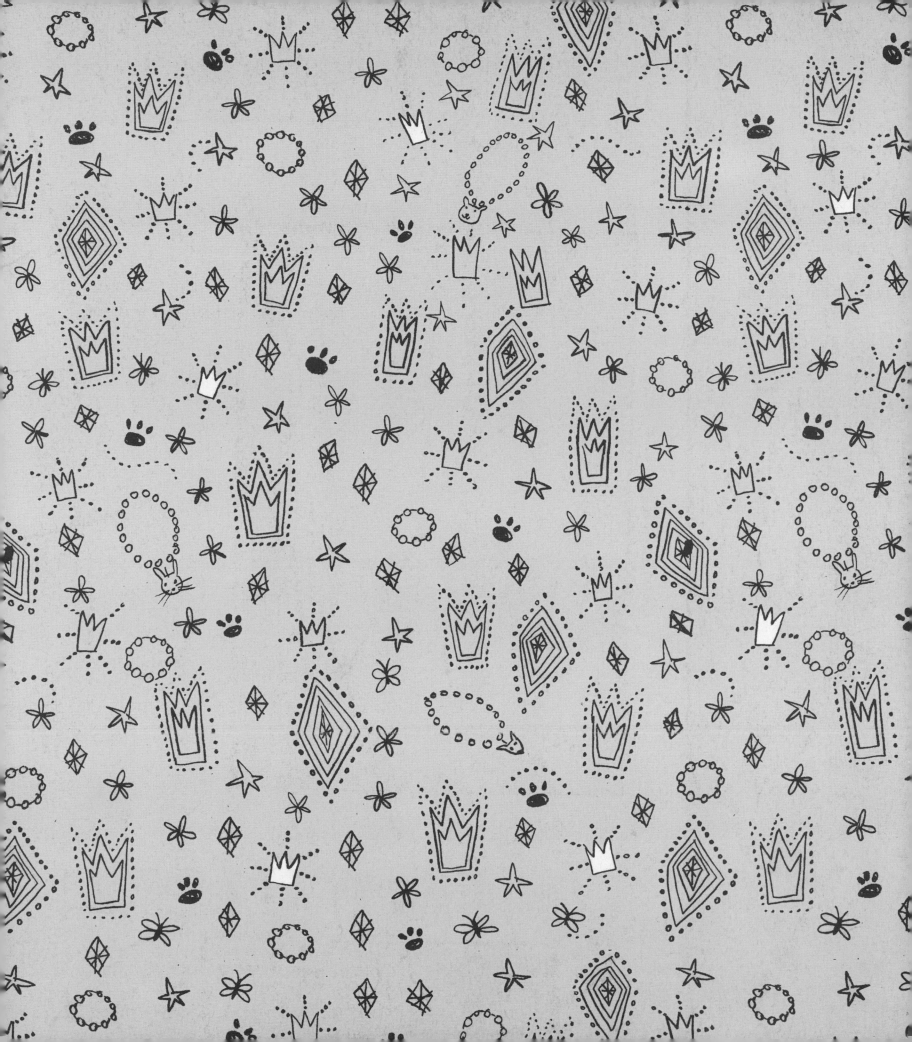

With love to dear Ruth — an inspirational lady! *C.F.*

For Jen — my royally super sister *A.P.*

First published in 2016 by Scholastic Children's Books
Euston House, 24 Eversholt Street
London NW1 1DB
a division of Scholastic Ltd
www.scholastic.co.uk
London ~ New York ~ Toronto ~ Sydney ~ Auckland
Mexico City ~ New Delhi ~ Hong Kong

Text copyright © 2016 Claire Freedman
Illustrations copyright © 2016 Ali Pye

PB ISBN 978 1407 14873 1

The moral rights of Claire Freedman and Ali Pye have been asserted.

Papers used by Scholastic Children's Books are made
from wood grown in sustainable forests.

Teeny-Weeny Queenie

By Claire Freedman

Illustrated by Ali Pye

SCHOLASTIC

CROWN JEWELS

Hello, Dear Loyal Subjects!
My name is *Queenie*, and I have a very BIG plan.
When I grow up I am going to be

Queen.

"You can't BE Queen," says my little sister Ella. "Mummy says you have to be BORN Queen."

"Ella," I sigh, in my most queen-like manner, "I was born *Queenie* — so that counts!" Daddy laughs and says, "If TEENY *Queenie* wants something she usually gets it!"

Because growing up can take *forever*, I have already
begun practising being queenly — to hurry things along.
I always carry my *Royal Handbag* with me.
Inside, I keep my Important Royal Treasures.

Sweets — to hand out to
Dear Loyal Subjects.

A *silver comb*—
a queen has to look her best
at all times.

MY RULE
BOOK

My *Royal Rule Book*
(to write important queenly decisions).

A *lace hanky* for my
delicate royal nose.

And, of course, my
Special Stately Tiara.

"Mummy!" I say. "You can be my Lady-in-Waiting!"
"Yes, *Your Majesty*," Mummy raises her eyebrows at me.
"Would Her Majesty like a drink?"

I give my queenly nod.

"Mummy," I sigh, "You forgot to curtsy.

ME

And next time please bring my biscuits on a *silver platter!*"

One day, my Lady-in-Waiting has a brilliant idea. "Why don't you invite some friends round for a *royal tea party*?"

I am SO excited. Right away I find my royal paper and begin writing out *majestic invitations* to my best friends, Emily and Rose.

"Are you going to write Ella
an invitation?" Mummy asks.

"No!" I say. "She'll spoil
our fun by being babyish!"

"*Queenie!*" Mummy frowns. "That's not very nice.
A *real* queen would care about **each** of her subjects —
not just her favourite friends."

I have a little think about this, because
a queen *does* listen to her royal helpers.
I decide to invite Ella after all.

During the week, my Lady-in-Waiting helps me
to get everything ready for my *royal tea party*.
Ella and I have great fun baking cakes, especially
the licking-the-icing-out-of-the-bowl part.

(I am not sure if a *real* queen would do this,
but I am in training, so it's allowed!)

"Daddy!" I say. "Your job at the tea party is to be my Special Royal Footman!"

"As *Your Majesty* wishes!" Daddy laughs with a deep bow.

At last, it's the day of the party, and Rose and Emily arrive.
"Tea will be served in the garden," I announce.

My Lady-in-Waiting hands round the tiny iced cakes,

but my Footman is not behaving at all royally!

"One simply **cannot** get good staff nowadays!"
I sigh to my friends.

After tea, we decide to make *Royal Crowns*.
Everyone's busy with paint and shiny paper
– except Ella. I *knew* it!

She's too young for royal games!

But then I remember what my Lady-in-Waiting said.
I take a deep breath, and try my very **queenly** best.
"I'll help make your crown, Ella," I say.

Soon I am caught up in such a royally exciting dressing-up game with Emily and Rose, I don't even notice Ella playing with the paints. Actually, I forget about her completely.

I don't see the paint pot she drops, either.

I go flying in a very un-queenly way!

"Look what you've made me do, Ella!" I cry.
"My beautiful *Royal Tea Party Dress* is totally spoilt!
I *knew* I shouldn't have invited you!"

I know it's not really my little sister's fault,
but I am SO upset.

"Queenie!" Mummy calls me.

Oh dear!

"Ella is only small," Mummy begins. "You are not being at all kind to her."

Suddenly I don't feel *queenly* at all.
I feel horrible and mean.

So I make a royal decision.

"Ella!" I say kindly. "Would you like to wear my crown for our **Royal Crown Parade?**"

"*Ooh*, yes!" smiles Ella happily.

Ella is majestic in our
Crown Parade game!

Then we have lots more fun together, playing *Stately Hide and Seek.*

Time rushes by, and soon Rose and Emily's parents arrive to take them home.

"Thank you for a lovely tea party, *Your Majesty,*"
Rose and Emily smile, with a curtsy. What Dear Loyal Subjects!

Then, to my complete surprise, Ella runs up and gives me a HUGE hug. "Thank you for the *best* party ever, *Queenie!*" she says.

Do you know what? At that moment I feel SO happy because
I know I have behaved like a *proper queen*, and that's what counts!

But best of all, I have a *royally* SUPER little sister.

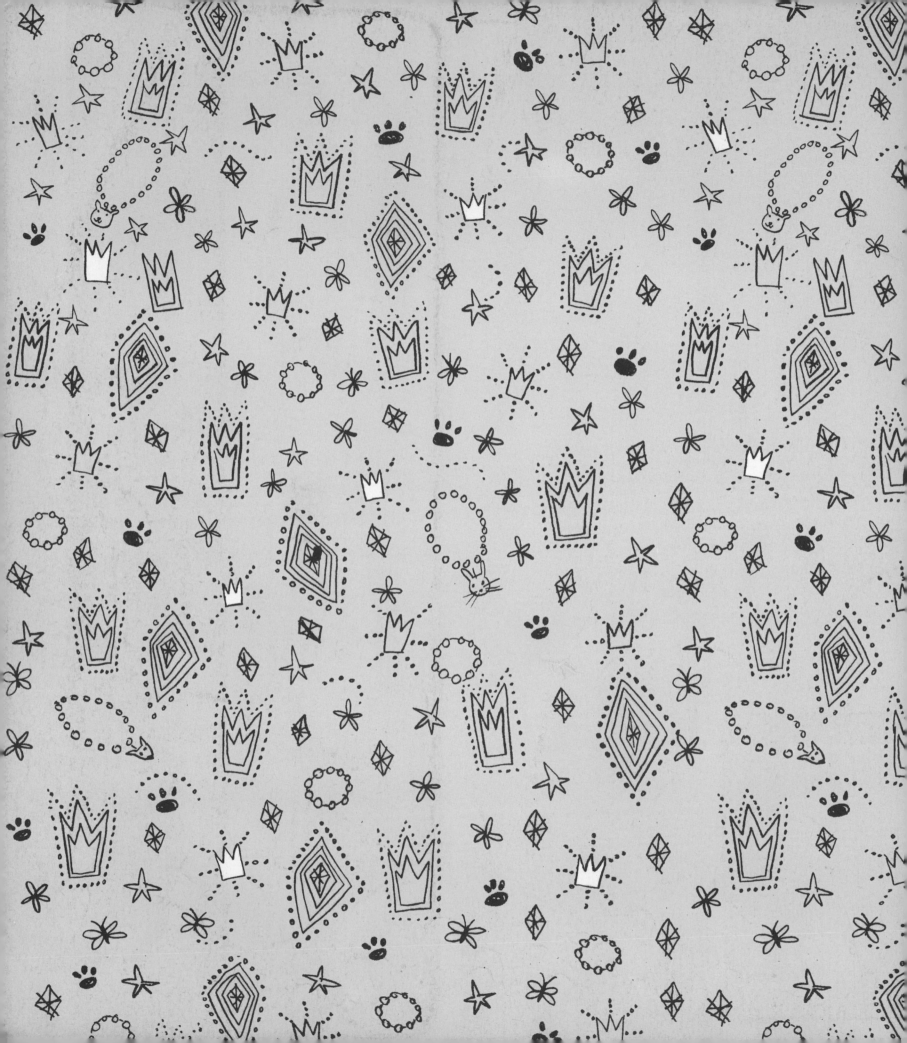